This Is the Matzah

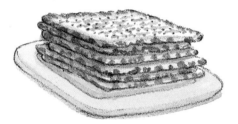

WRITTEN BY **Abby Levine**

ILLUSTRATED BY **Paige Billin-Frye**

Albert Whitman & Company

Morton Grove, Illinois

In memory of Rabbi Alan Bregman and
many happy family Seders—A.L.

For Diane Cloutier—P.B.-F.

Thanks to Emily Soloff of the American Jewish Committee. A.L.

By Abby Levine and Paige Billin-Frye
This Is the Dreidel
This Is the Matzah
This Is the Pumpkin
This Is the Turkey

Also by Abby Levine
Daddies Give You Horsey Rides
Gretchen Groundhog, It's Your Day!
Ollie Knows Everything

Library of Congress Cataloging-in-Publication Data

Levine, Abby.
This is the matzah / by Abby Levine ; illustrated by Paige Billin-Frye.
p. cm.
Summary: Rhyming text and illustrations describe the activities of a young boy and his family as they celebrate Passover. Includes facts about the holiday.
ISBN 0-8075-7885-1 (hardcover)
[1. Passover—Fiction. 2. Seder—Fiction. 3. Judaism—Customs and practices—Fiction.
4. Stories in rhyme.] I. Billin-Frye, Paige, ill. II. Title.
PZ8.3.L576Tgm 2005 [E]—dc22 2004018586

Text copyright © 2005 by Abby Levine.
Illustrations copyright © 2005 by Paige Billin-Frye.
Published in 2005 by Albert Whitman & Company,
6340 Oakton Street, Morton Grove, Illinois 60053-2723.
Published simultaneously in Canada by Fitzhenry & Whiteside, Markham, Ontario.
All rights reserved. No part of this book may be reproduced or transmitted in any form or by any means,
electronic or mechanical, including photocopying, recording, or by any information storage
and retrieval system, without permission in writing from the publisher.
Printed in the United States.
10 9 8 7 6 5 4 3 2 1

The design is by Carol Gildar.

For more information about Albert Whitman & Company,
please visit our web site at www.albertwhitman.com.

About Passover

Passover (in Hebrew, *Pesach*, pronounced PEH-sock), is an eight-day holiday that comes in March or April. It celebrates the exodus of the Israelites from slavery in Egypt over three thousand years ago. To recall how the enslaved Israelites fled before their bread had time to rise, nothing made with yeast—like bread or cake—should be eaten during the eight days. Instead, Jews eat matzah, like the flat, unleavened bread the Israelites made on their flight from Egypt. (Today's machine-made matzah looks different.)

On the first two nights, there is a dinner called a *Seder* (SAY-duhr). "Seder" means "order" in Hebrew, and everything that takes place follows an established pattern. A special plate contains foods with meaning for Passover. The celebration starts with a blessing over wine (for the children, grape juice), the first of four cups that will be poured. Parsley dipped into salt water is eaten. Three pieces of matzah have been placed in a cloth envelope in the center of the table. The middle piece is removed and broken in half. One half is returned to the cloth, and the other, the *afikomen* (a-fee-KOH-men), is hidden.

The youngest child asks the Four Questions, which begin, "*Mah Nishtanah*" (MAH Nish-TAH-nah). The Hebrew words mean, "Why is this night different from all other nights?" The questions lead to the telling of the Passover story, which each person reads in turn from a book called the *Haggadah* (Hah-GAH-dah). Special foods are eaten, including matzah, bitter herbs, and a sandwich made of bitter herbs and a sweet apple-nut mixture. Then the festive meal begins.

It is a custom to fill a cup for the prophet Elijah, who, according to tradition, visits each home to drink from the cup and give his promise of redemption to the Jewish people. A door is left open for Elijah to enter, and children check his cup to see if he has drunk.

After the meal, the children hunt for the afikomen; the finder gets a prize. Then songs are sung celebrating this festival of freedom.

This is the matzah stacked in the aisle.
Max reaches up to the top of the pile.

M

atzah for sandwiches, matzah for snacks,
for matzah meal brownies—and Seder," says Max.

The Seder Plate

Along with matzah, these foods symbolize the holiday.

maror (mah-ROR): a bitter herb like horseradish for the bitterness of slavery.

beitzah (BAY-tzah): a roasted egg for the new life of spring.

zeroa (zeh-ROH-ah): a roasted lamb bone for the lamb the Israelites sacrificed the night before they fled Egypt.

haroset (chah-ROH-set): a mixture of apples, nuts, and wine, which stands for the mortar the Israelites used as they labored for the pharaoh.

karpas (KAHR-pahs): often parsley, for the new leaves and growth of spring. It will be dipped in salt water, a reminder of the tears the slaves shed.

hazaret (chah-zeh-RET): another bitter vegetable, often Romaine lettuce.

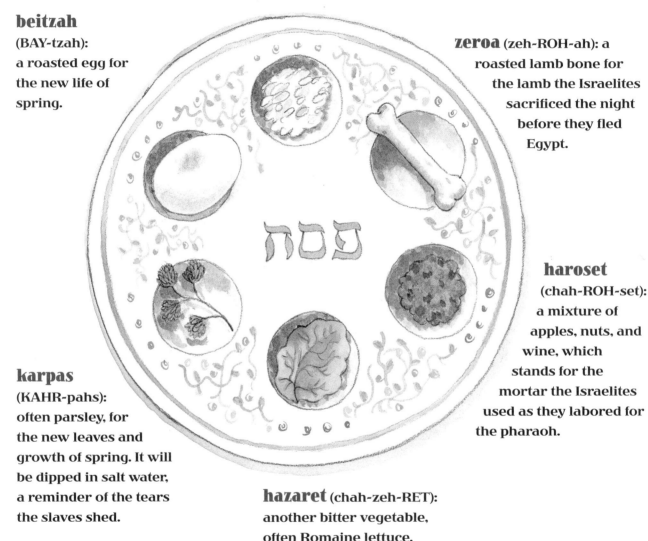

The Hebrew letters on the Seder plate read **Pesach** (PEH-sock), or Passover. The Israelites were spared the tenth plague (the death of the firstborn) when the Angel of Death *passed over* their houses, which they had marked with lamb's blood.

This is still early, but Ruth can't wait.
Max helps her to fill up the Seder plate.

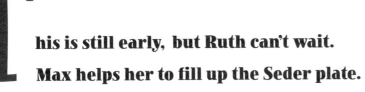

T

his is the tablecloth, spotlessly white,

the silver and goblets, sparkling and bright,

for this night so different from all other nights.

And for Elijah, this is his cup.
We fill it with wine—will he pick it up?

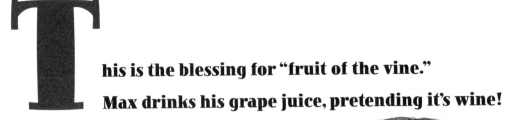

This is the blessing for "fruit of the vine."
Max drinks his grape juice, pretending it's wine!

This is the parsley we dip, for the years

we labored in slavery and shed salty tears,

after the blessing for "fruit of the vine,"

when everyone's sipped from the grape juice and wine

that sit on the tablecloth, spotlessly white,

for this night so different from all other nights,

where Ruth placed the beautiful Seder plate

that she filled up early (she just couldn't wait!),

next to the matzah, stacked in a pile

from boxes Max chose in the Passover aisle.

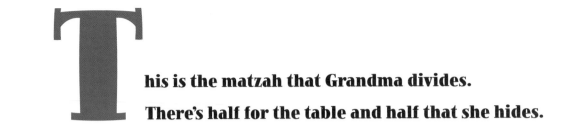

This is the matzah that Grandma divides.
There's half for the table and half that she hides.

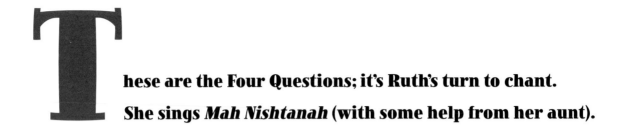

These are the Four Questions; it's Ruth's turn to chant.

She sings *Mah Nishtanah* (with some help from her aunt).

Blood · Frogs · Lice

Wild Beasts · Cattle Disease · Boils · Hail · Locusts · Darkness · Death of Firstborn

PASSOVER HAGGADAH

This is our story; each one tells a part.
(Max knows the names of the plagues by heart!)

In Egypt we toiled long and ceaselessly.
Moses asked Pharaoh to let us go free.
But hard-hearted Pharaoh refused to relent—
until the terrible tenth plague was sent.

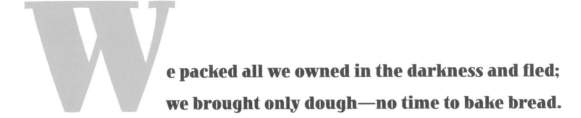

We packed all we owned in the darkness and fled;
we brought only dough—no time to bake bread.

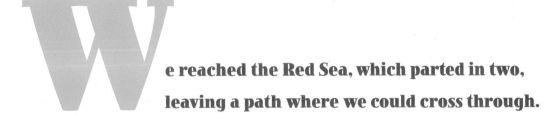

We reached the Red Sea, which parted in two,
leaving a path where we could cross through.

Our dough baked to matzah beneath the hot sun.

That day in the desert, it fed everyone.

Tonight we imagine that *we* are that band,
rescued from slavery by God's outstretched hand.

T

his is the sandwich of bitter and sweet.

And this is our dinner! It's time to eat!

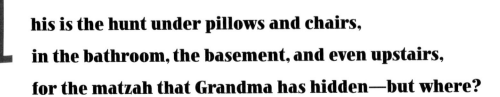

This is the hunt under pillows and chairs,

in the bathroom, the basement, and even upstairs,

for the matzah that Grandma has hidden—but where?

his is the door that Max opens wide.

He whispers, "Elijah, please come inside."

This is the wind that blows through the door.
Isn't it open now more than before?

Was it Elijah? Look at his cup!
We know he's been here, for he's drunk some wine up!

This is the uncle who sings out of tune
and louder than anyone else in the room,
after the wind has blown through the door
where Elijah has passed, as so often before,
and all the kids searched under pillows and chairs
for the matzah that's hidden—but no one knows where,
after the sandwich of bitter and sweet,
the story we tell before we all eat,
the parsley, the wine, and the table so bright
on this night so different from all other nights . . .

This is the end of our Seder—and then
tomorrow we'll start eating matzah again!

There's matzah lasagna that's served piping hot,
matzah balls bobbing inside the soup pot,
matzah meal brownies and matzah for snacks—
"We've got lotza matzah for Pesach!" says Max.